SNOWFLAKE

Kenny O'Connell

Acknowledgements

For my children, Erin, Elise, Chris & Carl, and granddaughters, Primrose & Poesy also my wife Sue, for her love and support in writing this book.

Jeff O'Connell, Illustrations.

(For other work by Kenny O'Connell, follow the link below)

http://www.oconnellmusic.co.uk/film_tv.shtml

ISBN 978-1-4710-3319-3

THE MEETING

Poland, December1944. Rumbling tanks plough their way through deep slush. Marching behind are foot soldiers with their rifles at the ready. As they come upon a small farmhouse, movement from a hedge alerts them. The soldiers spring into action and run forward, shouting out, jabbing their bayonets into the bushes. On finding nothing, they look over the top of the hedge into a small garden and see footprints in the snow. The soldiers force their way through the heavy thicket and track the footprints, leading them up to the front door of the farmhouse. They kick the door open and charge inside, splitting up to search every room.

"There's no-one here," shouts one of the soldiers as they make their way out from the house and fall back into line behind the tanks. The sound of the marching army fades into the distance…

The evening drew closer, and flying gracefully above was the Good Fairy; she was returning home after a long and disappointing trip to Hollywood. She had delivered a storming audition for the lead role as the Good Fairy in a new Disney movie. To her astonishment, she failed the audition and consequently spent the following hours trying to convince herself that the true meaning of art is to become someone else, to portray one's self would be fickle, which she was certainly not. She regretted her rash impulse for the glitz and glamour of Hollywood and scolded herself as she journeyed on through the cold winter's night. Through a break in the clouds, her eyes were drawn to a flickering light down below. Her instinct to investigate was strong, compelling her to land.

As she touched down, her bare feet made a soft crunching sound in the snow, she flapped her silver wings gently, sending particles of ice cascading to the floor. Her green-tinted eyes widened in surprise at the sight of a small child holding a glowing lantern, standing perfectly still by an open wooden hatch, buried in the ground.

The Good Fairy slowly approached and looked into the soft brown eyes of a nine-year-old child who was flicking snowflakes from her long neatly plaited brown hair, she was dressed in a woollen coat and black leather boots.

"Who are you?" asked the Good Fairy, looking concerned.

"My name is Snowflake," she replied, through icy breath.

"That's a pretty name, but surely it's not your real name...?"

The question made Snowflake quiet and withdrawn; she started walking in circles, making prints in the crisp snow.

The Good Fairy pressed her hands together in prayer-like fashion and asked caringly, "Where are your parents, do they know you're out here all alone?"

"Of course, they do, they're with me now," cried the little girl, smiling and twirling around with outstretched arms. "My Father is disguised as the wind, you can't see him of course, but I can feel the closeness of his breath as he swirls around me, keeping me safe."

The Good Fairy watched inquisitively as Snowflake's smiling eyes were drawn to the silver sky above.

"My Mother is a beautiful cloud, if you look closely, you can watch her changing shape, allowing rays of sunlight to sneak through and warm me. She dresses up every evening, and sometimes she even makes the moon blush!"

"Does she indeed…?" smiled the Good Fairy,

breaking Snowflake's artistic flow…

"And," added Snowflake with a huff, "when the night is clear, she hides behind the dark sky and watches me through the silvery stars that she calls her secret eyes; or so she told me before she and father went away."

"I'm sorry, what do you mean?" asked the Good Fairy.

"Well," said Snowflake in a sad voice, "wicked soldiers came and took my Mother and Father away on a train, but before they were captured, my parents hid me inside that small bunker and covered it with snow, saying they would always watch over me and protect me. So, when the wind blows, I'm not cold, neither am I afraid, as I know it's my Father surrounding me with his love; and when I see the beautiful shapes in the clouds and catch the falling snowflakes in my hands, I know it's my mother showering me with her love."

The Good Fairy welled up inside as she suddenly realised the little girl's parents had been taken to the death camps. She wondered how she could help the child, but before she had a chance to speak, Snowflake stepped forward with a curious look on her face.

"Who are you? What's your name? Where did you get those pretty wings and that sparkling dress?"

"What question shall I answer first?" smiled the Good Fairy.

"Your name, please," giggled Snowflake.

"This may come as a surprise to you, young lady, but I don't have a name; I am the Good Fairy."

Snowflake's eyes widened as her mind started racing. "You're the Good Fairy, you can bring my parents home, you can do anything," she said, laughing and dancing around, filled with excitement.

The Good Fairy replied tactfully, "I will help you search for your parents, but you must realise we may never find them. I mean, they could be, as you say, the wind and the clouds that serve in the sky above." Snowflake paused and looked up at her with a twinkle in her eyes. "My… what an imagination you have, Mrs Good Fairy."

"Well then, maybe I have the imagination of a child,"

replied the Good Fairy, more than impressed at Snowflake's wit. She then looked towards the open bunker next to the run-down farmhouse and asked, "How long have you been hiding here?"

"I'm not sure."

"How do you get food?"

"I sneak into the local village, soldiers are always passing through, but I'm much too quick for them," said Snowflake kicking her feet in the snow.

"I'm sure you are."

"So, you'll help me?"

The Good Fairy reached out to Snowflake taking hold of her hands, they rose up into the sky, leaving a trail of stardust behind them.

THE JOURNEY

Snowflake's eyes were wide with excitement as she gazed at the moonlit sky, asking, "Can we fly through the clouds? I want to be close to my Mother."

"Yes, and perhaps your Father can carry us along as only the wind can," replied the Good Fairy playfully. So, on they went, flying through the night sky, they were greeted along the way by a tapestry of silver stars painted across a dark blue canvas with a silver moon taking centre stage. On and on they voyaged until they glided into a cloud of black smoke, Snowflake coughed and rubbed her eyes, struggling to see. Without hesitation, the Good Fairy took action and diverted them away from the fumes into a clear sky. The scene down below was one of destruction, there was nothing but the charred remains of burnt houses and vehicles.

"Do you think there will ever be peace on earth?" asked Snowflake innocently.

"I pray every night that there will be, but I don't really know," said the Good Fairy, feeling uneasy with the subject.

"You don't know? I thought you knew everything and you could make the world whole; you are the Good Fairy, aren't you?"

"Yes, but I can only help people who do good."

"That settles it then because I'm a good person and so are my parents; so, finding them shouldn't be a problem," said Snowflake, gazing contentedly at the stars. The Good Fairy was worried, what if her parents weren't alive? How could she explain it to the child?

"This is the worst part of this job," she said to herself, sullenly.

Without warning, Snowflake shivered with excitement, squeezing the Good Fairy's hand at the sight of a flock of migrating geese flying alongside them, giggling, Snowflake reached out trying to touch the flapping wings. The birds let out an angry cry, the Good Fairy pulled Snowflake out of arm's reach, informing her, "There's a highway code up here young lady; obstructing the flight of birds is forbidden." The Good Fairy gave an apologetic look to the geese which they rejected and swiftly swung away in a fury.

Snowflake was oblivious to the Good Fairy's words, she was too busy living the dream. Yes, she was Peter Pan and Tinker Bell, all her heroes rolled into one; she was flying high, and nothing was going to stop her from finding her parents. She marvelled at the beauty of the moon casting light upon the earth, allowing her keen eyes to patrol the scorched ground below. Snowflake focused in on a group of weary-looking men, huddled together around a campfire and tugged at the Good

Fairy, pointing downwards.

The Good Fairy and Snowflake landed quietly out of sight behind a tree, they gathered themselves and approached the group of men.

"Excuse me," shouted the Good Fairy, "have you seen a Mr and Mrs err…" she turned curiously to Snowflake and asked, "what are your parents' names? If we are to find them, it would be a great help if we knew the names of the people we're searching for!"

"Well my Father's name is Alfred, and my Mother's name is Rachel, and we are the Isaac family," she declared, proudly raising her head.

"No, I haven't heard of them around here," replied an old man, struggling to stand up.

"There must someone who can help us?" asked the Good Fairy.

"You could try one of the camps set up by the allied soldiers further down the road; they may be able to help," said the man throwing wood onto a blazing fire.

The Good Fairy took a downbeat Snowflake by the hand and rose up into the air, frightening the life out of the men, who scurried away in terror. Snowflake covered her mouth, chuckling as they made the sign of the cross, looking upwards with terrified faces.

Soaring through the sky and weaving in and out of clouds, the Good Fairy looked questioningly at Snowflake, asking her, "well then, Miss Isaac, why do you call yourself Snowflake, is it a nickname?"

"Not really," replied Snowflake, her mind now reliving happier times with her parents. The Good Fairy looked on, waiting eagerly for a reply.

"My parents told me to use it when the troubles spread to our village; they said I must never use my real name," sighed Snowflake sadly.

The Good Fairy took a deep breath and turned her head away, gently squeezing the child's hand. As they travelled on, the night sky became darker, heavy clouds barged into each other and blocked out the moon and stars. Snowflake's eyes became alive with wonder as a shooting star streaked across the skyline and dropped like a flaming arrow to the ground.

"Where did he go?" asked Snowflake.

"He's burnt himself out," said the Good Fairy, firmly clutching Snowflake's hand and picking up speed as they flew over the mountain tops. A cold wind was making flight difficult, and the Good Fairy could see that Snowflake was getting tired and hungry, so they started to descend...

THE HOUSE

Smoke curled out from the chimney pot of a secluded house located behind a cluster of scorched trees, a dim light shone through the half-open curtains.

This would be the perfect place to rest, thought the Good Fairy, her spirits now lifting. "Let's hope somebody is at home," she said to Snowflake as their feet softly touched the ground.

There was a sudden movement in the window of the house; the light flicked off - the curtains were swiftly closed. Snowflake looked up at the Good Fairy, frowned and edged up close to her. The Good Fairy put her arm around Snowflake's shoulders and guided her towards the front door. Just as she raised her hand to knock, the door opened slowly, and a man popped his head out, staring them up and down with suspicion. The Good Fairy was about to speak when he cut her short.

"Take your business elsewhere; I have enough strife of my own."

"But, please," begged the Good Fairy, "this child is tired and hungry; surely you can afford one simple act of kindness by letting her rest, at least until morning?"

"There is no morning, afternoon or night for me. The war is coming to an end, and this house is not the safest place to be, so be gone with you woman."

"Don't you dare talk like that to the Good Fairy!"

snapped Snowflake, stamping her foot on the ground. The man looked down at her with a heavy frown. "Good Fairy! If there was such a thing, people wouldn't be suffering all around us," mocked the man, shaking his head and letting go a bitter laugh.

The Good Fairy looked long and deep into his eyes as if she were reaching out to his lost soul. The man took a step back; his expression changed, his eyes went to the cold white face of Snowflake, and with a wave of his hand, he motioned them into the house.

They entered a tiny living room that was lit by a bare, hanging light bulb; the floor was strewn with empty beer bottles, scrunched up balls of paper and dirty ashtrays. Placed in front of a small coal fire was a stack of knotted papers. The man knelt down and started to place them onto the blazing fire.

Snowflake took off her boots and put her feet close to the fire-grate, wiggling her toes.

"That feels lovely and warm," she said, smiling at the man who gave a strained smile back to her as his mood began to change.

Looking over the man's shoulder, the Good Fairy enquired, "Why are you burning those papers?"

He replied with a haunted look, "When the war started, I made a pact with the Devil; the lives of my wife and children in exchange for information. I knew the day would come when I would have to pay my debt to God; I have no allies, only enemies."

The Good Fairy looked sadly at the man as he turned away, staring vacantly into the flames of the blazing fire.

"Do you know if Mr and Mrs Isaac passed through here?" asked the Good Fairy.

"You mean, Alfred and Rachel Isaac?" countered the man, rising up from the floor.

"Yes! Yes! They're my parents," shouted Snowflake, jumping around in front of him. The man looked wistfully at Snowflake and walked towards a wooden cabinet. Opening the top drawer, he pulled out a folder and started searching through documents.

"Nothing here," he said, shoving the folder back into the drawer. He picked up the stack of papers by the fire and started sifting through them. The Good Fairy held onto Snowflake's hand in anticipation. The man's eyes narrowed as he read a document. "Here we are," he cried, shaking out a piece of paper. "They were taken south to a camp not too far from here; I know some people survived there. You can rest for the night and start out first thing in the morning if you like?"

The Good Fairy looked at the tired face of Snowflake, who smiled excitedly, nodding her head.

"We gratefully accept your offer Mr..?" said the Good Fairy, waiting for a reply…

"You don't need to know my name," said the man, placing the paper on the table. He walked towards the window and opened the curtains slightly and peered out into the yard. His misty eyes focused in on a broken swing and a small bike that lay half-buried in the snow. His mind replayed a thousand memories. He snapped out of his trance and smiled for a few seconds, and then tears filled his eyes. The Good Fairy, for once, felt lost; she didn't know what to do or say, but Snowflake did; she ran up to the man and took his hand, squeezing it gently, smiling up at him.

"How many children do you have?"

"Four," replied the man in a broken voice, taken aback by Snowflake's actions.

"Are they boys or girls?"

"Two boys and two girls," he said, as a smile lifted his face.

"Where are they now?"

"Somewhere safe, I hope."

"I'm sure they are," said Snowflake, picking up a rag-doll from a basket, that belonged to the man's daughter. He smiled as Snowflake cradled the doll in her arms, rocking back and forth, whispering a lullaby.

Snowflake had taken down the barrier; the man now spoke freely, as if he'd been released from some invisible prison. They sat together, drinking hot chocolate and eating toasted bread as he showed them photographs of his wife and children. Snowflake made him laugh and clap in admiration as she displayed her dancing skills. The shared warmth was quickly broken when from the backroom, the shrill sound of breaking glass brought stillness and quiet.

The man spun around, searched through a drawer and pulled out a gun.

The door flew open and a stranger, dressed in military clothes, burst in and grabbed Snowflake by the hair. He dragged her into the corner of the room and pressed the barrel of a gun to her head.

"Andros, let go of the child; she knows nothing," pleaded the man.

"Give me what I need and give it to me now!" demanded Andros, his eyes shifting from side to side.

The Good Fairy made herself invisible.

Andros gazed around, confused, trying to figure out where she had gone. "Show yourself, or I'll kill the child," he screamed.

The Good Fairy appeared before him; her face filled with fear.

"Don't shoot," said the man, placing his gun down on the floor, "I'll give you what you want." The man moved swiftly to the cabinet and picked out a folder, handing it to Andros, who looked through it quickly and then shoved it under his arm.

An evil calm came over Andros as he stared coldly around the room. "Leaving evidence would be foolish," he said in a callous voice, spinning the chamber of his gun.

"Please no, let the child live, she can do you no harm," pleaded the man, moving bravely forward. Andros pulled his pistol away from Snowflake's head and pointed it at him. "Stay back," warned Andros as he started to squeeze the trigger, but before he could finish his act of evil, Snowflake elbowed him in the stomach as hard as she could, causing the gun to go off, blowing a hole in the wall.

The man charged at Andros, smashing him into the cabinet, he tried to wrestle the weapon from his hand, but Andros was too strong and threw him across the floor, he cocked his gun and took aim at Snowflake.

The man sprung up from the ground and hurled himself in front of the child, taking the full impact of the bullet. Again, Andros raised his gun and pointed it at Snowflake, but before he could pull the trigger, a shot rang out…

The man had retrieved his handgun and found the strength to fire off a round, saving Snowflake. Andros slumped back against the wall, dropping his weapon to the floor. Clutching his wounded shoulder, he picked up the folder and fled through the back door.

Snowflake knelt down by the side of the man, resting her hand on his chest. He reached up, touching her cheek gently, smiling with relief, knowing she was safe. He then wiped a tear from the child's cheek before his hand fell lifelessly to his side. Snowflake broke down and turned to the Good Fairy, pleading, "Please, help him. You can do it; you can do magic."

"I can't," choked the Good Fairy, "I can only help good people, and this man has done wrong, so I am powerless."

"He just did a great thing," sobbed Snowflake, pointing at the bullet wound, "he gave his life for me."

The Good Fairy was upset and confused by the child's words; would she be breaking the rules? Of course, she would, but without question, this man had redeemed himself and deserved another chance at life.

The Good Fairy cleared her mind of all negative thoughts and moved Snowflake to one side. She opened the man's shirt, exposing the bullet hole in his chest and started circling her hand over the dead man's wound, Snowflake looked on, wiping tears from her eyes as each second passed. From the fingertips of the Good Fairy, a stream of blue light appeared and connected to the wound. Slowly but surely, his injured chest began to heal, but the man remained still and silent. The Good Fairy looked at Snowflake fearfully before placing her hand onto the man's rib cage, gradually he began to breathe, his upper body rising and falling. Snowflake's face lit up as the man's eyes slowly crept open, with tears of joy rolling down her cheeks, she hugged the Good Fairy.

The man clambered to his feet in a dazed and confused state. He looked down at his chest where he had been fatally shot and declared. "A miracle has happened." Touching his healed body and reaching out to the Good Fairy, he gasped, "how can I ever thank you?"

Making eye contact with Snowflake, he paused in deep thought. He then spoke apologetically in a soft voice, "Child, your parents were the last ones to leave, I did my best for them whilst they were held in this house."

Snowflake shrugged her shoulders, "Why didn't you just let them go?"

"They would have killed my family; don't hate me, please," beseeched the man, shaking his head.

"I don't hate you," replied Snowflake, rising to her feet, "I think everything is going to be alright."

"So, do I," said the Good Fairy, placing her arm lovingly around Snowflake's shoulders.

Snowflake motioned to speak, but stayed silent as a look of relief came across the man's face. He sat in silence for several minutes and then walked unsteadily across the room and opened a cupboard door; he reached into an old tattered suitcase and pulled out a map, he scribbled down directions and handed it to the Good Fairy. "You must leave tonight," he said in a serious voice, "it would be too dangerous to wait for the morning light, but please be careful, Andros is dangerous; some say he possesses evil powers."

"Evil powers?" gasped the Good Fairy.

"Yes, so keep out of sight until you reach your destination."

"Will we see you again?" asked Snowflake, tugging on the man's arm.

"I hope so," he replied, gently patting her head. The man passed through the front door, pausing outside on the pathway. Snowflake and the Good Fairy followed him.

"Tonight, you have both changed my life forever," said the man, putting his suitcase on the floor, before he could say another word, Snowflake surged forward and hugged him.

"I don't deserve that," he said in a choked voice, embracing Snowflake.

The Good Fairy looked the man in the eyes, smiled, and nodded a 'yes'. As he picked up his suitcase and turned to walk away, Snowflake called after him, "Your name, what is your name?"

"Michal… Michal Leski," said the man smiling and waving goodbye.

The Good Fairy and Snowflake stood watching as he made his way down a dirt track.

"Do you think he'll find his family?" asked Snowflake.

"I know he will," said the Good Fairy.

Snowflake smiled in delight, the Good Fairy took her by the hand and led her away from the house.

THE CALLING

Before another word could be spoken, the Good Fairy and Snowflake took to the air and headed south towards the camp that Michal had pointed out to them on the map. They travelled for the next thirty minutes in silence, giving each other the occasional sad smile. The moon was now in full glow as the horizon became clear. On the ground below they could see campfires and people moving about.

The Good Fairy swung to one side, sweeping Snowflake along with her; they flew down and landed safely. The Good Fairy remembered what Michal Leski had told her; she was now a bit more cautious about rushing into unknown situations.

They walked warily along the road on which debris and empty shell cases were scattered, making use of any available cover along the way. The Good Fairy pulled Snowflake closer and placed a protective arm around her as the crackling of burning wood from a fire up ahead could be heard.

They were drawn towards the sweet sound of the song, "Adon Olam" being sung by a skeletal-looking man in a tattered striped uniform clinging weakly to a wire fence.

Snowflake's eyes widened as she went up on her tip-toes, "That's my Father singing," she shouted excitedly to the Good Fairy, "doesn't he have the most beautiful voice?"

"He certainly does, but why on earth he's singing is beyond me," remarked the Good Fairy, looking around at the devastation.

In no time at all, Snowflake was in her father's arms crying with delight. "Oh, Father, where is Mother?"

"Look behind you, my child."

Her mother stood, smiling through tear-filled eyes, she reached out, and Snowflake ran forward, jumping up into her arms.

"Amelia, my baby, I thought I'd lost you forever," cried her mother.

"I thought you and Father had left me."

"We hid you in the bunker covered with snow hoping you'd be safe there. We prayed someone would find you and look after you."

"They did, Mother, I was helped by the Good Fairy."

"My child, there are no such things as fairies."

"Yes, there is Mother," said Snowflake, turning round to look for the Good Fairy, but she was nowhere to be seen. "Mother, Father," said Snowflake eagerly, "She brought me here, we flew through the air, we teased the wind and brushed along the clouds making them prettier than they've ever been."

"My child," said her mother, "what an imagination you have."

"What does it matter?" said her father, hugging his daughter, "We are back together now."

Snowflake was about to answer when Andros sprung out from the shadows, his face twisted in anger. As blood flowed from his wounded shoulder, he cupped it into his hand and let out an evil chant, flicking it onto the earth which started to rumble as the night became darker than one could ever have imagined.

Snowflake was petrified and held onto her parents who watched in dread as the ground opened up, and a dark, evil figure appeared staring at them through wild, green eyes, breathing fire. The Demon started to move towards Snowflake and her parents. She looked to her Mother and Father, who fell to their knees, terrified and too weak to resist the darkness that stood before them. Snowflake shouted out for the Good Fairy to help them, but there was no answer. The Good Fairy had gone.

Snowflake bravely tried to raise her parents up onto their feet, but it was useless, they were too frail. She turned around in circles looking up to the sky with her arms outstretched, crying out once again to the Good Fairy, "Why have you left me? Please give my parents the strength to protect us." Snowflake could see the Demon getting closer, she looked once again to the sky for the Good Fairy.

Snowflake's eyes widened, she gazed in disbelief as a cluster of stardust shot across the sky and disappeared inside a cloud hanging above them. Her mother stared up in hope as the cloud began to change shape, she squeezed Snowflake's hand tightly as the cloud fell from the sky and smothered the Demon whilst it struggled and fought with all its might. It twisted and turned, screaming in anger and frustration… as the seconds passed it started to free itself from the grip of the cloud. Andros lunged forward, flicking blood onto the Demon, making it stronger.

Snowflake clung onto her parents, shaking with fear as the Demon drew near. Mister Isaac rose to his feet in an attempt to face the force threatening them. Snowflake tried to scream, but her breath was snatched away by the roar of a mighty wind that began to bend and sway large oak trees.

Her father wrapped his arms around his wife and daughter as the wind turned and ripped through the backwoods, breaking branches and spraying leaves high up into the air. Changing course, the wind dropped down with great force, encircling the cloud and spinning it round and round. With an almighty gust, the wind swept the cloud away, trapping the Demon and Andros inside. The evil force screamed out in defeat as it was carried up and away into the cold, dark sky.

Snowflake jumped up in delight, holding both her parents as closely as she could. "Oh, Mother, you're softer than the clouds, and Father, you're stronger than the wind; nothing can hurt us now."

Everything became peaceful and still. The sky turned into a silver mask; the distant sound of church bells rang out. The fingers on the church clock struck midnight, and snow began to fall.

Amelia's eyes lit up, and she smiled as a single snowflake melted through her fingers.

Allied soldiers and released prisoners walked side by side, singing songs of celebration.

Her mother, who was still shaking, held her daughter close, telling her the war was over.

Snowflake knew that when she looked up at the clouds and felt the wind against her face, the Good Fairy would be watching over her.

www.ingramcontent.com/pod-product-compliance
Ingram Content Group UK Ltd.
Pitfield, Milton Keynes, MK11 3LW, UK
UKHW020215250726
13967UKWH00001B/5

9 781471 033193